First published in the UK by HarperCollins Children's Books in 2009

1 3 5 7 9 10 8 6 4 2

ISBN 13: 978-0-00-730390-8

Licensed by:

Printed in Great Britain by Clays Ltd, St Ives plc

ANIMATED™

Time-Quake

HarperCollins *Children's Books*

Strange things have been happening in the city of Detroit. All the news channels have been talking about it. Time is out of control!

People have been late for events all over the city. It's as if time were moving at a different speed in some areas. Minutes have been stretched to feel like hours for some people, while elsewhere, hours have gone by in a flash.

The mayor has assured everyone there is no need to panic – but you can tell that everyone is nervous. A top team of scientists are working around the clock to discover the cause of the time distortions.

Some people have blamed the Autobots. You heard one of your teachers talking about it earlier at school.

'Ever since the Autobots showed up here, there's been nothing but trouble,' you heard one of your teachers say.

'But they always sort it out, don't they? They are heroes,' another teacher had replied.

Your teacher just snorted. 'But that's my point. The Autobots have lots of enemies – and when they fight them innocent people get caught up in their battles. Like this time-quake business. I bet it's connected to the Autobots – or one of their enemies.'

This afternoon you experienced the weirdness for

yourself. Something very strange happened during the last lesson of the day; one moment the lesson had just started and then, suddenly, it was going home time.

All your friends thought it was brilliant, but you want to know why it happened. On your way home you wonder if your teacher was right. Is it something to do with the Autobots?

Without warning an alarm goes off somewhere nearby.

If you run to see what has happened, turn to 12.
If you try to ignore it, turn to 26.

Before Bulkhead can disappear inside the building someone comes running out of it.

It's a man, wearing an old-fashioned military uniform and carrying a primitive-looking musket.

You realise you've seen men wearing this kind of uniform before, in history books.

'What devil's mischief is this?' cries the man, wide-eyed and fearful.

'Don't be scared,' says Bulkhead, reassuringly.

'What are you?' cries the man, bringing his ancient musket up into a firing position. 'A speaking mechanical! Is this some British trickery?'

Now you realise where the man has come from.

'The Revolutionary War! You're a Minuteman, aren't you?' you ask the man.

'I fight for the rights of all Americans,' says the man. 'No taxation without representation!'

'Can you tell what year this man is from?' asks Bulkhead.

If you provide Bulkhead with an answer, turn to 36.
If the man answers himself, turn to 55.

Bulkhead shakes his head. 'It's not good, I've tried that already. There's too much air pollution and interference from unshielded electrical equipment. It's making it hard for me to function at optimal efficiency,' he confesses.

A little girl and her father walk past you, and the girl stops to admire Bulkhead.

'Cool robot,' says the girl, grinning at you.

Her father grabs her hand and pulls her away hurriedly.

'Come on, Natalie, don't stare,' he says, casting an apprehensive look back at Bulkhead.

Suddenly you hear a blast of horns from the nearby road. A teenage girl is running across the street between the traffic.

'Bulkhead – help!' you shout out. The girl is now bending over to pick something up from the road surface, completely unaware of a bus that is about to flatten her.

If Bulkhead grabs the runner, turn to 33.
If Bulkhead stops the bus, turn to 68.

You look around and realise that you are safely back in the 22nd century.

Bulkhead asks if you're okay.

You tell him that you think you're getting used to time travel now, but when you try to move, your legs buckle.

Bulkhead moves quickly and catches you.

'I think that temporal transport is very disruptive for organics,' Bulkhead tells you, 'it's quite uncomfortable for Autobots too.'

'Does it make you dizzy, too?'

Bulkhead nods. 'It scrambles my circuits, if that's what you mean?'

You put the two control balls back on the plinths where they belong.

As if it was waiting for the balls to be put back in position, the machine's lights fade a little and its hum drops down in pitch.

If the machine is in a warehouse cellar, turn to 71.
If the machine is in a penthouse suite, turn to 38.

One of the men takes a step towards you.

'What was that you said about the "sons of liberty"?' he demands, waving a tomahawk in your face. Close up, you see that the dark smears on his face are indeed coal dust.

'No need for that,' says Bulkhead, stepping forward and plucking the Indian-style hatchet from the man's grasp. He crushes the weapon between two massive fingers. 'You should be careful carrying something like that around, someone could get hurt.'

The man looks up at Bulkhead in disbelief.

'Wh-what is that thing?' he asks you, frozen to the spot with fear. 'Have the British summoned a demon to stop our tea protests?'

'He's a friend, not an enemy,' you explain. The man sees the control ball in your hand.

If the man tries to run from you, turn to 32.
If he grabs the ball from you, turn to 67.

To your amazement, standing at the end of the street is a powerfully built caveman. He is dressed in furs and covered in filthy mud. His hair is long and matted with dirt. The most noticeable thing about him however is not his appearance; it is his stench. He smells awful, like the city dump on a hot summer's day. Wherever he has come from, it must be from a time before they invented baths.

He looks angry and disorientated. His thick-boned skull is creased in a permanent frown.

He roars, grunts and begins running towards you.

Now you realise why all the people were running away.

You look around for help but the street is empty.

'Over here, kid,' shouts a voice.

If the voice seems to come from an abandoned SWAT car, turn to 90.

If you can't work out where the voice comes from, turn to 56.

Bumblebee tells you that you need to go to the top floor – that's where all the weird energy signals are coming from.

Bulkhead walks up to the sliding doors of the building. Nothing happens. The doors stay firmly shut.

Bumblebee zooms around Bulkhead and reaches the door ahead of him.

'Allow me,' he says and directs two short energy bursts at the door mechanism.

There is a small explosion, some smoke and then the huge doors slide open silently.

Once inside the building, you hurry across to the massive service elevators and jab at the call button.

A lift appears and the three of you step inside. You notice there are no buttons for individual floors, but press the 'up' button anyway.

If the lift goes up, turn to 74.
If the lift goes down, turn to 104.

'You seek an object like the one you hold?' asks Benjamin Franklin.

'Yes, have you seen one?' you ask.

Benjamin Franklin nods.

'I have been on the hills lately. I am waiting for a suitable storm to test my theories of electricity. Recently there was a very unusual occurrence. A storm of lights that came and went in moments and with no rainfall. My son alerted me to the phenomena and I ran to see, but was too late. But at the spot where my son had seen the lights, I found an object just like that one.'

Bulkhead steps closer to Franklin.

'Where is it now?' he asks.

'At my home here in Philadelphia, as I plan to study it further.'

If Benjamin Franklin invites you to his house, turn to 82.
If you ask to see the device, turn to 52.

The heat mist clears and you see that a creature has materialised on the sidewalk. It has huge sharp tusks and angry eyes and looks a bit like a hairy elephant. It is a creature from another time – a woolly mammoth.

It lowers its head and begins to charge.

You find yourself rooted to the spot, unable to move.

Bumblebee zooms in front of you, firing energy bolts at the maddened creature, which slow it down. Ratchet uses his magnetism to pluck a street lamp from the ground and throws it to Prowl. Prowl, able to turn anything into a weapon, throws it like a javelin and hits the mammoth directly on the forehead.

The giant creature falls to the ground unconscious and immediately fades away back to the past.

In the confusion you manage to get yourself into the building and head for the tenth floor.

Turn to 58.

'This is madness,' mutters the man, wide-eyed, as he stares at you and Bulkhead. 'What is this thing? Some armoured machine made by the Yankees to try and smash the Confederate Army? I've never seen the like.'

You can't help but smile. 'It's just a robot,' you tell him. 'This is Detroit – Bot-City U.S.A. We have robots here to do everything. Get you coffee. Do your chores. It's great.'

The man begins to nod. 'Slaves. Is this the future? Mechanical slaves?'

Bulkhead bristles at this description. 'We're not exactly slaves – we do have our freedom.'

The Confederate soldier frowns. 'Are you saying that the Yankees will eventually triumph?'

You look at Bulkhead realising that you need to be careful how you answer this time traveller's question.

The Autobot is busy checking some readings on a scanner.

If Bulkhead detects an energy spike, turn to 31.
If the soldier disappears, turn to 87.

The figure stepping through the door is a woman. She's dressed in a tight grey suit and has long dark hair. Her eyes are a very dark shade of blue.

'Please step away from my equipment,' she demands in a cool voice.

'I'm sorry ma'am,' says Bulkhead, 'but I'm not sure I can do that.'

'My name is Natasha Pyraniac and that machine belongs to me,' the woman tells Bulkhead in the same cool tone. 'So please stand aside now.'

'Do you have any idea what that machine does?' asks Bumblebee, his curiosity getting the better of him.

The woman shoots him a look cold enough to freeze running water. 'Of course I do. I made it. Now let me through or suffer the consequences.'

Bulkhead and Bumblebee both laugh.

If the woman starts laughing, too, turn to 81.
If the woman calls in a friend, turn to 63.

You run down the street in the direction of the alarm. Smoke and fire are pouring out of a second floor window of an old building on the corner. Broken glass and debris lie on the street underneath the window.

You hear distant sirens, but the emergency services are yet to arrive.

Suddenly a vehicle appears, screeching around the corner and skidding to a halt in front of the burning building. It is a massive heavy duty SWAT car, and you wait, expecting the doors to burst open and a swarm of well-armed police officers to appear – but nothing happens.

It's almost as if the SWAT car itself was looking at the building and thinking.

If you go up to the vehicle, turn to 86.
If you decide to wait and watch, turn to 41.

Without warning someone steps out of the shadows and runs rings around the pair of you at impossible speeds. All you can see is a smear of yellow and the sound of laughter.

Bulkhead shoots an arm out – CLUNK!

You look down and see Bumblebee, the smallest and fastest of the Autobots, lying on the floor, nursing a sore head.

'You didn't have to do that,' he complains, getting to his feet, 'I was only having some fun.'

'We're not here for fun,' Bulkhead reminds him sternly. 'We're looking for some kind of time machine.'

'I might be able to help you with that,' Bumblebee says. 'This empty building is not quite as empty as it ought to be.'

If he tells you that you need to go to the top floor, turn to 7.

If he tells you that he has found a way in, turn to 34.

It still feels strange deep inside your stomach during the instant of time travel.

Soon the white light has disappeared and you are in the past again. You see that you and Bulkhead have arrived on a hillside.

You spot a figure climbing up the hill. He is dressed in knee-length breeches, long white socks and has shoes with a large metal buckle.

Bulkhead opens a panel in his arm and begins to take a reading.

'Tell me youngster, is this some metal automaton?' asks the stranger.

'Actually, he's an Autobot,' you tell the man, and then introduce yourself.

The man shakes your hand. 'Benjamin Franklin, delighted to make your acquaintance.'

'Pardon my curiosity, but what powers the script on that glass paper?' he asks, pointing at the screen set into Bulkhead's arm.

If Bulkhead answers, turn to 70.
If you answer, turn to 60.

You follow Bulkhead into the building and see a figure emerging from the smoke inside.

It is a wild-eyed man wearing some kind of red military uniform and in his hands he is holding an old-fashioned musket.

He can't seem to believe his eyes as he sees Bulkhead advancing towards him.

'What monstrous mechanical is this? An iron man with a semblance of life?' stutters the frightened man.

'There's nothing to be scared of,' you tell the man, but you can see that he isn't really listening.

'Is this some trickery by King George?' he asks.

You realise that this man is a Minuteman – fighting to repel the British who ruled America from afar during the American War of Independence.

'This man has fallen through time,' says Bulkhead, 'but what year has he come from?'

If you provide Bulkhead with an answer, turn to 36.
If the man answers himself, turn to 55.

'You have lost an item similar to that which you hold in your hand?' asks Benjamin Franklin.

'Yes,' says Bulkhead, 'have you seen one?'

Benjamin Franklin shakes his head.

'I cannot say that I have,' he tells you.

'Are you sure?' you ask him. 'It is very distinctive with its five buttons.'

'Five? Surely three –' Franklin begins and then trails off. 'I apologise friends, but like my associate George Washington, I cannot tell a lie. I have indeed seen such a device. I wanted to conceal the matter from you so I could satisfy my own curiosity, but I'm afraid deceiving people is not in my nature.'

'So you found a ball like this one? With three buttons?' you ask.

'Right here on this hill not two days ago,' Franklin answers you.

If Benjamin Franklin invites you to his house, turn to 82.
If you ask to see the device, turn to 52.

Lincoln turns and calls to his aides who are standing with the crowd next to the monument.

'Mr Williams, can you please fetch the artefact?' President Lincoln asks.

The man dashes off.

'I was up late, working on this speech last night when I was treated to a most unique light show. Afterwards my aide and I found the twin to that which you hold.'

The aide returns with the sphere and gives it to you. You hand it to Bulkhead who has been waiting patiently. The President is shocked to see him move.

'I thought it a strange kind of statue,' he mutters.

'Thanks,' says Bulkhead, 'but I prefer to look at statues than to be one!'

If the sphere Bulkhead is holding lights up, go to 78.
If the sphere you are holding lights up, go to 42.

Suddenly, Bulkhead puts a hand to his helmet.

'Incoming message,' he tells you. 'I'll put it on loudspeaker.'

The voice of Optimus Prime fills the room.

'Autobots, I have located the chrononaut and his captor. The time traveller has been imprisoned by a Decepticon named Wavelength. He's holding the time traveller at a quay a little way south from your location. I want you to meet me there as soon as possible. Transform and Roll Out!'

The two Autobots instantly head for the street.

'What about me?' you call after them. 'I've been back in time with you – I'm part of this mission, aren't I?'

Bulkhead and Prowl stop and look back at you.

'The youth has been with me all through this adventure,' says Bulkhead.

If Bulkhead says you can ride with him, turn to 47.

If Prowl says you can come with him, turn to 66.

You feel a strange vibration in your hand and the sphere you are holding begins to glow.

You look across to Bulkhead and see that the one he is holding is doing something very similar.

'What's happening now?' you ask.

'They seem to be reacting to each other,' Bulkhead says. 'Better get ready for another trip through time.'

'But how are we going to stop the time-quakes?' you wonder.

'Prime has a theory,' Bulkhead tells you, 'he believes that anything out of time in the past would send disturbances through the space time continuum, making holes in time.'

'So if we stop that happening there'll be no more quakes...' you conclude.

You feel a peculiar sensation wash over you and realise that you have travelled in time again.

**If you have only visited one time zone so far, turn to 50.
If you have visited two different time zones now, turn to 4.**

You can no longer see the rest of the room, as a bright blue light covers you, forming a curtain between you and Bulkhead – and the rest of reality. You have a sensation you are sinking into the floor as if it were made of shifting sand or soft snow, but, as you look carefully at your feet, you now see that the intense white light of the floor is actually rising up from the ground and sliding up your body. The wave of bright headache-inducing light moves swiftly, up over your knees, your hips, your chest...

As it moves there is a strange sensation, like a line of pins and needles and a flash of heat and then the light is passing up your face and you close your eyes.

A moment later, all sensation is lost and you feel wind on your face.

You open your eyes.

To your great relief Bulkhead is still by your side.

'That rattled my circuits,' he confesses. 'I wonder where and when we are now?'

You look around and take in your surroundings. You are no longer inside the building where you found the time machine. There is a sidewalk underneath your feet and a roar of traffic from nearby. But the vehicles on these roads are not the robot controlled electric cars of 22nd century Detroit. These are old fashioned petrol-driven motor cars. The smell is awful.

Around you are lots and lots of tall buildings, not dissimilar to those you know at home. But the noise and pollution here are very noticeable.

Bulkhead takes a reading. 'I can't say how far we've travelled,' he tells you.

If you tell Bulkhead where you are, turn to 97.
If you tell Bulkhead where you are, turn to 97.
If you ask someone, turn to 43.

You lead the way across the room towards the mysterious machine.

'Is it some kind of time machine?' you wonder.

'It's certainly connected to the time distortion energy that we've detected,' Bulkhead tells you.

You take a closer look at the machine. It is a bulky bit of equipment with massive metal arms covered in wires curving over a central platform. Behind the platform is a row of metre-high stands. On top of most of these you can see what look like metal baseballs.

You take a step on to the platform and pick up one of the balls to take a closer look. It is inset with some buttons and other controls.

The machine begins to hum in a rising pitch.

Bulkhead climbs on to the platform to join you.

If you begin to sink into the ground, turn to 91.
If you are enveloped in bright blue light, turn to 27.

There is a sudden distortion in the air and you feel a blast of intense heat. Flashes of colour appear, sparkling and dancing in a mini-tornado. As quickly as it blew up, the time storm calms down and, when the dust settles, there is a human figure lying on the ground where a moment ago the street was empty.

As you and Bulkhead watch in fascination the man begins to get to his feet. You notice he is wearing a military uniform.

'The uniform is of a soldier in the Confederate Army,' Bulkhead tells you, 'I've seen it in paintings in galleries.'

You gasp. 'You mean from the time of the American Civil War!'

Bulkhead nods. 'Somehow he's travelled three hundred years through time!'

If the man attacks you, turn to 102.
If he speaks to you, turn to 10.

Bulkhead tells you to hide behind the machine.

Meanwhile Bumblebee darts around the Decepticon firing off energy blasts at rapid speed.

The enemy 'bot, already disorientated from Bulkhead's shockwave is knocked one way then the other. Falling to the floor the Decepticon grabs a loose girder from the floor above and throws it at Bumblebee.

The little yellow Autobot leaps into the air and manages to jump clear of the solid metal girder. The Decepticon is just warming up though; he throws more and more debris at Bumblebee forcing him to jump and twirl, bend and duck, to avoid the makeshift missiles.

'Bravo!' shouts Bulkhead. 'Best ballet I've seen in ages!'

The Decepticon realises he has been ignoring Bulkhead. Slowly he turns to look behind him.

If Bulkhead is standing there, turn to 79.
If there is no one there, turn to 105.

A shape forms in the mist and suddenly there is a massive horned dinosaur standing in front of you. You recognise it as a Triceratops – a vegetarian.

'It's okay,' you call out to the Autobots, 'it's not a meat-eater.'

'How does it feel about metal?' wonders Bumblebee, as the frightened creature lowers its head and begins to charge.

With its central horn and two further tusks higher on its skull the creature is clearly dangerous.

Ratchet pulls a truck into its path with his magnetic powers, but the Triceratops rips through it as if it were made of paper.

Luckily, Bumblebee can now set off a series of energy bolts and manages to bring the creature down but then, without warning, the dinosaur just fades away.

During the fight, you slip unnoticed into the building and take the lift to the tenth floor.

Turn to 58.

'Mr Lincoln?' you shout. 'President Lincoln?'

The man looks up and it is President Abraham Lincoln, sixteenth president of the United States of America.

'My apologies, I did not see you there,' he tells you.

You see he is holding a much folded piece of paper.

'I didn't mean to disturb you,' you say, 'I can see that you are busy.'

'A few words for the dedication ceremony,' he mutters, 'nothing of great significance.'

'Wait a minute, where is this?' you ask, remembering a comic book history of America you read at school.

'Why this is Soldier's National Cemetery in Gettysburg, of course, to be dedicated this very day.'

You realise that Lincoln is about to give his most famous speech.

If you ask him about his speech, turn to 51.

If you ask him about the metal spheres, turn to 93.

You ignore the alarm and carry on walking towards the hover-tram stop where you will catch your ride home. As you walk, you realise the sound is getting louder.

You turn a corner and find a crowd of people and robots coming running towards you.

'Run for your life!' screams a woman, as she hurtles past you. You flatten yourself against a wall as the hordes run by.

After a few moments the stampede has passed and you are alone again.

You watch as the last of the frightened people disappear around the corner.

You hardly dare look back to see what they were running from.

You turn your head and gasp in astonishment at the incredible sight before you.

If you can see a dinosaur, turn to 44.
If you can see a caveman, turn to 6.

You can no longer see the rest of the room. You are surrounded by a bright blue light and a thick mist. It looks like it should be cold but there is a warmth to the fog that surrounds you. A rectangle of white light, the same dimensions as the platform you stepped on is rising up your body, giving the sensation you are falling through the floor.

When the light passes over your head everything goes dark for a moment and when you blink, you are somewhere else.

You look to one side and are relieved to see Bulkhead looming over you.

You look around, looking for clues to your location, both in space and in time.

You're at a harbour filled with sailing ships of all sizes. It is getting dark. You and Bulkhead are standing in a small alley between two wooden buildings on the quayside.

You see some men moving along the harbour wall. They pass a sign pointing to Griffin's Wharf. The men are dressed in a peculiar fashion. They seem to be wearing Native American costumes and are carrying tomahawks. They have dark smudges on their faces.

Bulkhead makes an adjustment to his optical sensors. 'The men appear to have coal dust on their faces,' he tells you. 'Could they be miners?'

'I think I know who they are and where we are,' you tell him with a smile. 'I saw a TV programme about this at school. This is Boston, December 1773, these men are the Sons of Liberty.'

The metal control ball that you are holding begins to bleep and flash a blue colour.

If one of the men spots you, turn to 5.
If Bulkhead gets the ball to stop flashing, turn to 98.

Slowly Bulkhead raises one of his powerful legs from the floor, keeping his gaze fixed on the Decepticon the whole time. Blast-X returns the look, his eyes locked on Bulkheads. It's like two cowboys about to have a duel – except only one of them has a weapon.

Suddenly the two cowboys go for their guns. Bulkhead slams his foot down – hard, on the floor. At the same time, Blast-X unleashes his power blast.

The thunderous stamp from Bulkhead's foot has sent a shockwave along the floorboards, causing Blast-X's aim to go high as he loses his footing.

The power blast hits the ceiling, causing a small avalanche of plaster and debris. A curtain of tiny particles seem to cut you off from the rest of the room.

Bumblebee takes advantage of the cover and zooms off at high speed.

If Bulkhead tells you to hide behind the time machine, turn to 23.
If Bumblebee attacks Blast-X, turn to 103.

Blast-X lets out a scream of fury. 'Noooo!'

Bumblebee fires off a couple of his stingers but Blast-X hits back with one of his sonic booms.

'Bulkhead!' calls Bumblebee, as he somersaults out of the way. 'I could really use a hand here.'

Bulkhead brings his two massive fists together to crush the enemy 'bot but Blast-X manages to evade the blow.

'You'll not catch me with that move,' he says, stepping back. 'I've seen every fight you've ever been in! That woman brought back data from the future on every one of you. I know all your strengths and weaknesses better than you do.'

He fires another blast of sonic energy at Bumblebee and Bulkhead knocking them both off their feet and steps forward ready to attack again. Bravely you step in front of him.

'Out of my way, organic,' he orders you.

'No, listen,' you insist. 'If you've seen all their battles from the future then you can't defeat them today because then they wouldn't have all those fights, and you wouldn't have them from the future to watch.'

Blast-X is still for a moment as the logic of your statement sinks in.

'It's called a time paradox!' adds a new voice – you look up and see that it is Prowl. He and the rest of the Autobots have arrived.

Ratchet, Prowl and Optimus Prime launch an attack on Blast-X. The enemy 'bot realises he doesn't stand a chance and turns to make a run for it but Bulkhead is waiting for him. CRASH! Bulkhead hits him right under the chin with one of his huge pile driver fists. Blast-X flies into the air and comes down with a crash.

'Didn't see that coming, did you?' jokes Bulkhead, standing over the defeated 'bot.

Turn to 106.

The dinosaur takes a step closer to you. You shrink back against the wall, wishing the wall will somehow absorb you and protect you.

Suddenly the SWAT car you saw begins to move. In a flash it completely changes itself from a vehicle into a big bulky two-legged robot. You recognise him immediately; it is one of the famous super hero robots from Cybertron – Bulkhead of the Autobots.

He picks up an abandoned taxi and throws it at the T-Rex.

'Pick on someone your own size,' he calls.

The taxi bounces off the back of the dinosaur which turns and roars at the Autobot.

'What's that?' says Bulkhead bravely. 'Did you want to say something?'

The dinosaur begins lumbering towards Bulkhead, bellowing in fury.

If you suddenly feel strange, turn to 40.

If you feel a blast of heat, turn to 64.

Bulkhead looks up. 'Energy spike. Imminent temporal disturbance. Stand back from him,' he tells you.

There is a sudden rise in the temperature and a wind starts up out of nowhere. The air begins to twinkle around the time-displaced man and there is a sudden flash of intense light and you shield your eyes.

Then, just as quickly as it began, the wind drops and the temperature returns to normal. You see that the time traveller has vanished.

'Has he gone back to where he came from?' you ask.

'I don't know, but I did get a good trace on the energy trail. I think I can track down the source.'

'So you can find the machinery that made the time-quake?'

Bulkhead morphs into his vehicle form.

If he suggests you jump in, turn to 100.
If he begins to drive off, turn to 89.

The man takes off, running back towards the quay.

'Wait!' you call after him, but he doesn't stop or even hesitate.

'I think he has seen one of these before,' you suggest to Bulkhead.

'Then we need to talk to him further,' says Bulkhead, 'wheels are quicker than legs, I'll get into vehicle mode and then we can catch him...'

'No, wait,' you reply, 'I think a SWAT vehicle roaring down the quayside might be a bit much for history to cope with.'

Bulkhead nods in agreement. 'Pity we can't all be Prowl, I suppose,' he mutters, then he picks you up and starts to run.

With his huge strides it doesn't take long for you to reach your target. Bulkhead grabs him with his free hand and plucks him into the air.

If the man faints in his hand, turn to 95.
If the man demands to be put down, turn to 83.

Bulkhead changes to his vehicle form, screeches across four lanes of traffic, turns back to his robot mode and grabs the youth. The astonished drivers of New York greet the daring rescue with a chorus of horns.

Bulkhead brings the grateful girl – who tells you her name is Gabriella Costanza – back to the sidewalk where she shows you what she was running to pick up – it's a metal control sphere.

You realise who Gabriella is. When she is older she will become the 47th President of the United States – the first woman President. If she had been killed trying to get the sphere, history would have been changed!

You explain that the sphere is an experiment that needs to be returned to a laboratory and she hands it over.

If the sphere Bulkhead is holding lights up, go to 78.
If the sphere you are holding lights up, go to 42.

Bumblebee reports that he has found a way into the building. Intrigued, you and Bulkhead allow him to lead you around to the side of the secured building.

He points up at a small window set at first floor level. Bumblebee and Bulkhead both look at you.

'Reckon you could get through there?' asks Bumblebee.

'Sure,' you hear yourself say with confidence.

'Here, let me give you a hand,' says Bulkhead, allowing you to stand on his robotic palm. Carefully, he lifts you up and a moment later, you're in. You quickly hurry down the main staircase and open the door for them, overriding the security system.

'Now what?' asks Bulkhead.

'We go up!' you tell him, heading for the service lifts. You pile into one of the larger elevator cars .

If the lift goes up, turn to 74.
If the lift goes down, turn to 104.

'I'm okay,' Bulkhead reports, standing up and shrugging off the debris.

The orange glow is coming from a massive piece of equipment, covered with wires, dials and valves. In the middle of the machine is a small metal platform. Next to this are six plinths with metallic balls sitting on top of most of them.

The two Autobots begin examining the machine. You investigate the platform and pick up one of the metallic balls and notice some control buttons. The machine begins to hum at a different frequency.

Bulkhead joins you on the platform.

'Be careful,' he says, but before you can put the ball back something very strange begins to happen.

'It's switched on,' you say.

If you begin to sink into the ground, turn to 91.

If you are enveloped in a bright blue light, turn to 27.

'1775. Am I right, sir?' you say, looking towards the confused man.

He looks at you and nods.

'In truth, it is the year of our Lord, seventeen hundred and seventy five. And my name is John Hawkins, of the Lincoln Militia Company. We ride to face the British at Lexington,' he tells you. He looks around him. 'But this is not Lexington, is it?'

You cast a glance at Bulkhead who has flipped open a panel in one of his forearms and is looking at some read-outs.

'If this guy had fallen through time, why is he in Detroit, not Massachusetts?' you ask.

'Temporal dislocation leads to spatial dislocation,' he says, without looking up.

'What?'

'Your planet's always moving,' Bulkhead points out, 'so if you move in time, you also move in space.'

If Bulkhead detects an energy spike, turn to 31.
If the Minuteman disappears, turn to 87.

Prowl tells you the machine fell through time from some point in the future where time travel has been perfected, possibly the 45th century.

'Did it come with a pilot?' you ask.

Prowl nods.

'We believe that there was a chrononaut – a time travelling explorer – with the machine but he was captured when he appeared and taken prisoner.' Prowl tells you.

'Taken prisoner by whom?' you ask, but Prowl only tells you that there are Autobots following some leads right now.

'Is it something to do with Megatron?' wonders Bulkhead.

'Not directly – but one of his people, certainly. A Decepticon we've not faced before perhaps.'

Prowl explains that Optimus Prime, Ratchet and Bumblebee have been investigating and he is expecting a message any minute.

If Optimus Prime makes contact, turn to 18.

If Bumblebee makes contact, turn to 54.

You are back in the skyscraper where you discovered the time machine with Bulkhead and Bumblebee – but Bumblebee isn't there anymore.

'Typical,' mutters Bulkhead, 'I guess he couldn't be bothered to wait for us.'

Without warning, a wall at the far end of the room explodes into pieces. Something yellow is thrown – with considerable force – right through the bricks and plaster.

Bulkhead moves with surprising speed and grabs hold of the disorientated Bumblebee with one hand.

'Looks like you need a hand!' he jokes, as he puts his friend down on the floor gently.

'Bulkhead! At last, I knew we shouldn't give up on you!' says Bumblebee.

'Something else isn't giving up,' you tell them, pointing towards the hole in the wall that Bumblebee just made where a figure is stepping through the dust.

If it is a Decepticon, turn to 72.
If it is a human, turn to 11.

Your stomach lurches and seconds later you realise you've moved through time again and are relieved to see Bulkhead is still with you.

He takes a look around, trying to work out where – and when – you are now.

You can see that there are rows of white gravestones laid out in semi-circles in every direction that you look. It is a graveyard, a cemetery, on a very grand scale.

You vaguely make out a small crowd gathering some distance away near a monument. Nearby is a man dressed in old-fashioned clothes, walking and talking to himself. You catch sight of his face and know him instantly.

If you call out the man's name, turn to 25.

If you stare at the man silently, turn to 84.

You feel a peculiar sensation in your stomach.

'What's happening?' you ask.

There is a blast of heat, a flash of light, and the street is empty once more.

'Fallen back through time?' you speculate.

'It seems likely,' Bulkhead agrees.

'So what's causing these time-quakes?' you ask. 'Are the Autobots on the case?'

'We're doing all we can,' Bulkhead tells you, consulting a scanner built into his arm. 'Looks like I've got a trace on the source of the temporal energy.'

'You're on your way to find whoever or whatever is mucking about with time?'

Bulkhead changes back into his vehicular form.

If he suggests you jump in, turn to 100.

If he begins to drive off, turn to 89.

As you watch from the shadows, the SWAT vehicle suddenly begins to vibrate. There is a strange alien noise of gears and metal moving and, incredibly, the vehicle morphs into a robot. You are looking at one of the famous Autobots!

'Bulkhead!'

You realise, with a shock, that it is your voice. Furthermore, the giant Autobot has swung his big metal head to look in your direction.

'Get away!' Bulkhead shouts. 'There is terrible danger here!'

'What kind of danger?' you ask. 'Is it something to do with the time-quakes?'

Bulkhead flips open a panel on his wrist and takes a reading.

'If by time-quakes you mean the temporal anomalies that have been occurring recently,' he tells you, 'then yes, it is to do with that. And there's about to be one right now.'

If someone appears, turn to 22.

If Bulkhead grabs you, turn to 65.

The sphere in your hand begins to light up and vibrate. The one that Bulkhead has starts to do the same. There is a sudden dimness to the light and your surroundings become almost transparent. Silence descends over you. You and Bulkhead are isolated in a tiny bubble of reality.

'I think I'm getting used to this time travel,' you say to Bulkhead.

'I wish I was,' he mutters, 'every time we do this it completely scrambles my sensors.'

'What did you do to start it happening?' you wonder.

'Nothing,' Bulkhead tells you, 'I think it must be some kind of automatic recall system.'

'It must be pre-programmed to a particular destination,' you say, 'so which will it be: past or future?'

Bulkhead shrugs, 'We'll soon find out.'

If you have only visited one time zone so far, turn to 85.
If you have visited two different time zones now, turn to 49.

'Excuse me,' you ask a man walking by, 'but where are we?'

The man looks at you as if you are an idiot. 'New York, of course.'

'And the year?'

'2012,' he tells you, 'what else could it be?' The man hurries off muttering something under his breath about tourists.

You give Bulkhead a grin. 'I guess New Yorkers are New Yorkers whatever the year!'

Bulkhead is looking at the control sphere he is holding. It is pulsing gently.

You look around. 'There has to be another one of these spheres in this time zone and this location,' he says.

'But how are we going to find something as small as that in a city the size of New York?' you wonder.

You have an idea.

'Try running a scan for the time energy?' you suggest to Bulkhead.

If Bulkhead tries your idea, turn to 92.
If Bulkhead shakes his head, turn to 3.

At the end of the street is a dinosaur. A massive Tyrannosaurus Rex. It stares at you and bares its teeth.

You start edging towards the corner, keeping your back to the wall and staring at the massive reptile in front of you.

'Keep still,' a voice calls to you.

You freeze, taking the advice, but have no idea where the voice came from.

There is no-one else on the street. Just a few abandoned cars. You notice that one of the driverless cars is a SWAT car. Even the police ran away!

If the dinosaur comes closer, turn to 30.

If the SWAT car moves, turn to 76.

'Bulkhead – damage report?' says Prowl.

Bulkhead stands up and then staggers a little.

'Minor damage to my gyroscopes,' he reports. For a moment he wobbles and then manages to stand straight. 'I think I can compensate,' he tells you, 'Ratchet can patch me up properly later. Come on then...'

Across the dark cellar is a large machine with a central platform. Around the machine is an arc of metre high stands. On the top of all but two of the stands are metal balls about the size of a baseball. Each has three indented buttons on it and a dial.

You pick up one of the balls to take a closer look and immediately the whole machine begins to make a sound like an engine warming up.

Bulkhead hurries to join you.

If you begin to sink into the ground, turn to 91.
If you are enveloped in a bright blue light, turn to 27.

The woman quickly steps on to the time machine platform and reaches for one of the control balls.

'What are you doing?' you demand, jumping up and grabbing her wrist.

'Get off me!' she shrieks and pushes you back off the platform. The machine begins to power up.

'Sorry to cut and run,' she says to you, pressing a sequence of buttons on the control ball, 'especially when we've had such fun. But I can see I've out-stayed my welcome in this primitive time.'

'Primitive?' you repeat.

'I come from your distant future,' she confesses. 'Technology gives us everything we can ever want. And it's so boring you wouldn't believe. I came to the past to have some fun. But the fun's over now so... time to go...'

With that, the woman and the entire time machine fade from view.

If Bulkhead speaks, turn to 88.
If Blast-X speaks, turn to 29.

Bulkhead tells you to come with him, and moments later you are riding in his cab as he speeds down the coast road to the rendezvous location.

Soon you are standing with all the Autobots outside a restaurant on a pontoon that sticks out over the river.

'Wavelength and the time traveller are in there,' Optimus Prime tells you, 'but we can't get inside. Wavelength stores a form of super-charged electricity and has used that to booby-trap all the doors. Whenever we try to enter, our circuits are scrambled.'

'Even at my top speed I can't get past the ring of shocks,' adds Bumblebee.

You look down at your feet and smile.

'These trainers I'm wearing have rubber soles,' you tell the Autobots.

'You think you can get past Wavelength's barrier?' says Bulkhead.

You explain your plan.

Turn to 53.

'This way,' says Prowl. He leads the way into the building. 'Be careful,' he tells you, 'there are holes in the floor.'

He shines a powerful torch beam across the warehouse. You can see an orange glow coming up from one of the holes.

'What's that?' you ask.

Prowl creeps carefully across to where the light is coming up from the basement and looks down.

'Some kind of machine,' he reports, 'we need to get down there and take a closer look.'

You look around for a stairwell.

Bulkhead thinks he can see a door leading to some stairs.

'Over here,' he calls and begins to cross the floor.

There is a sudden creaking noise, as if the floor is about to give way under his weight.

'Bulkhead!' you shout.

If Bulkhead falls through the floor, turn to 75.
If you fall through the floor, turn to 69.

You close your eyes, cross your fingers and when you open them, you are relieved to see you are finally back in 22nd century Detroit, standing on the time machine platform.

Bulkhead leans down to check you are okay.

'I'm fine,' you tell him, but then you feel a bit queasy and have to sit down.

'I think time travel must be pretty hard on your organic bodies,' says Bulkhead. 'It makes me feel like Ratchet's given me an upgrade and used old parts!'

Carefully, you put the control balls back in their places.

As soon as all the balls have been returned the machine's lights fade and it seems to power down.

If the machine is in a warehouse cellar, turn to 71.
If the machine is in a penthouse suite, turn to 38.

This time the sensation of travelling through time isn't quite as uncomfortable as it was previously. The feelings are the same but knowing how it works makes you less stressed about the process.

The now familiar bright light passes over you and, very simply, you are transported from one time and place to another. The question now is: where and when have you been transported to?

You take a look around and are immediately struck by the sounds of the city. You've not returned to the 22nd century but this is definitely closer to your time than your last destination. There are tall buildings around you, a paved sidewalk under your feet and roaring traffic nearby. The fumes from the cars are overwhelming. Wherever you are, they still use fossil-fuels as an energy source.

If you tell Bulkhead where you are, turn to 97.
If you ask someone, turn to 43.

'Is this the one that starts "Four score and seven years ago"?' you ask him.

He looks at you and then reaches in his pocket for a pencil. He makes a quick note on his paper.

'That's a fine turn of phrase, young man, I'll use that if I may.' He looks at the revised opening and nods. 'A much bolder opening: "Fourscore and seven years ago our fathers brought forth on this continent a new nation." Yes, much better... I am indebted to you.'

You wonder if you've caused some kind of terrible time paradox. You've used your knowledge of history to change the past. 'Perhaps you can do me a favour in return, Mr President?' you ask, and show him the metallic sphere. 'Have you seen anything like this before?'

If President Lincoln calls an aide, turn to 17.
If Lincoln steps closer and whispers, turn to 73.

'May we see the device?' you ask. 'It is potentially dangerous if it is not returned to where it came from.'

'Why, of course. Come with me now and I will give it to you,' says Benjamin Franklin. He then stops and takes a look at Bulkhead.

'It may be prudent, however, for your metal friend here to await your return in yonder woods. We do not wish to alarm my neighbours.'

Leaving Bulkhead safely hidden amongst the trees you set off to walk alongside one of the founding fathers of America. Eighteenth century Philadelphia is very different to Detroit four hundred years in the future.

At his house Benjamin Franklin is true to his word and hands over the control ball. You thank him and return to Bulkhead.

When you get there if the ball begins to glow, turn to 57.
If you give the ball to Bulkhead, turn to 19.

The Autobots aren't convinced by your plan but you tell them it is the only way.

Bulkhead picks you up and deposits you carefully on the roof of the one-storey building. Your rubber-soled trainers act as insulators, protecting you from the electrical current. Once on the roof you use the fire escape to get into the building itself.

You find yourself in the kitchen of the restaurant. You peek through the swing doors into the main dining area. You see a blue-coloured Decepticon standing over a pale man in strange clothing. The Decepticon's body is alive with little blue sparks of electrical current.

You look up at the ceiling which is covered with emergency fire sprinklers. You know that water and electricity don't mix so you find the control box and set off the sprinklers. Instantly water pours down and the Decepticon short-circuits. Now the Autobots can safely enter the building and cut off any chance of the Decepticon escaping.

Soon it is all over. The captured Decepticon is handed over to the police. The freed time traveller tells you that his name is Aron Three Five. He was visiting the 22nd century from the far future when he was attacked by Wavelength. The Decepticon's attempts to use the machine without understanding how it worked caused all the time distortions.

The Autobots reunite the time traveller with his machine.

Aron Three Five checks everything is running smoothly, adjusts some controls, then turns to say goodbye.

'Thank you for your help,' he says. 'I dare not tell you anything of the future in case I cause a paradox, but believe me, you Autobots are still remembered in the 51st century...'

He pulls a lever and the entire machine glows a bright orange and then fades from view.

YOUR ADVENTURE WITH THE AUTOBOTS IS OVER.

Suddenly there is a buzz of engine sound and you all run outside the building to see who has arrived. It is Bumblebee.

'Hi guys,' he says, 'Optimus Prime sent me to get you.'

'What's happening?' asks Prowl. 'Have the rest of you located the missing time traveller?'

'Of course we have,' says Bumblebee, whizzing around the three of you in his excitement.

'So it's all over,' you say.

Bumblebee screeches to a halt.

'Not exactly,' he confesses.

'Ratchet found the missing time traveller but we can't get to him. He's been kidnapped by a Decepticon called Wavelength. They're holed up in a riverfront diner a few klicks south of here.'

'I guess we'd better get down there and see if we can help,' says Prowl, 'transform and roll out!'

If Bulkhead says you can ride with him, turn to 47.
If Prowl says you can come with him, turn to 66.

The soldier looks at you and then at Bulkhead.

'It is the year of our Lord, seventeen hundred and seventy five,' he tells you.

'You're a Minuteman?' you gasp.

'Minuteman?' asks Bulkhead, flipping up a panel on his arm to reveal a small screen.

'They were fighters in the Revolutionary War,' you explain. 'We did a project at school on them. They were Militia men – trained soldiers who could be called up to defend America.'

The man nods. 'My name is John Hawkins of the Lincoln Militia Company. Tell me youth, is this Lexington?'

You shake your head in confusion.

'If he was in Massachusetts 400 years ago, how can he be here in Detroit now?' you wonder.

'The Earth moves,' explains Bulkhead simply, 'so if you travel in time, you travel in space.'

If Bulkhead detects an energy spike, turn to 31.
If the Minuteman disappears, turn to 87.

You cannot work out where the voice came from. In the meantime, the angry caveman is getting closer to you. You see that he is waving a heavy wooden club which has sharp stones set into its thick end. He is swinging the club around his head, like an athlete with a hammer. You suddenly remember what happens when the athlete lets go of the hammer, but it's too late as the deadly club is already hurtling through the air towards you.

A figure appears between you and the caveman and catches the club in mid-flight.

It is Bulkhead, one of the Autobot heroes that makes Detroit such a safe place to live.

Bulkhead holds the club in one hand and then smashes it to pieces with his other fist.

If you feel something peculiar inside, turn to 40.

If you feel a blast of heat, turn to 64.

The metal control ball in your hand begins to glow. The one Bulkhead is holding begins to do the same thing.

'What are they doing?' you wonder.

'I think they are activating a temporal shift,' says Bulkhead. 'We're going to travel in time again.'

'Are you sure?'

'I'm getting the same kind of sensor readings as before,' Bulkhead explains. 'There must be some kind of automatic recall.'

'And was this the cause of the time-quakes?' you ask.

'We don't know,' Bulkhead confesses, 'but we think so. An out-of-time device like this could create disturbances in the space/time continuum.'

You feel a strange sensation and then everything around you begins to become faint, as if covered in thick mist.

If you have only visited one time zone so far, turn to 39.
If you have visited two different time zones now, turn to 4.

When you reach the tenth floor you find a man sitting in front of a bank of TV monitors. On the screens you can see images of different locations around the building, including the sidewalk in front of it where the Autobots are.

The man is middle-aged and is wearing a white lab coat. As you walk up behind him he runs his hands through his hair and groans.

'Why can't you just leave me alone?' he wails, talking to the screens. You see that the Autobots are making another move towards the entrance.

'I can't keep sending things to stop you – all this time travel takes a lot of energy.'

'Then just give yourself up,' you suggest gently, hearing the desperation in his voice.

The Professor swings around in his seat and looks at you in astonishment.

'Who are you?' he demands.

You explain who you are and repeat your suggestion that he give himself up. For a moment you think he is going to argue but then his shoulders sag and he sighs heavily.

A little while later, it is all over. The Autobots have arrived, secured the location and alerted the authorities. Professor Hawkins tries to explain.

'I just wanted to use the time travel technology to help people. I thought that farming animals from the past might solve the problem of global hunger,' he explains. 'Instead every trip I made to the past ripped a hole in the fabric of space/time and I had to spend all my time and energy getting rid of displaced people and creatures that had fallen through time. Every time I tried to make it better, it got worse.'

You almost feel sorry for him as the police arrive to take him away but then you remember all the damage that he had caused.

Turn to 106.

Prowl tells you that the machine was constructed by a local Detroit Scientist.

'Professor Simion Hawkins from the Detroit Institute of Advanced Technology, to be precise. He published some research about possible methods of time travel ten years ago but the scientific community rejected his ideas and called him a fool. Since then he has been a recluse.'

'But he carried on his work on time travel?' you suggest.

'It appears so.'

'So where is he now?' asks Bulkhead.

'We've been tracking down spikes of temporal energy all over the city,' Prowl explains. 'The rest of the Autobots have got a site under observation downtown.'

'So what are we waiting for?' you ask. 'Let's go...'

Prowl is not sure you should be allowed to go.

Bulkhead tells him that you deserve to.

If Prowl says you should go with him, turn to 62.

If Prowl agrees you can ride with Bulkhead, turn to 80.

'It is a form of electrical energy,' you tell the man.

Franklin is immediately excited. 'That is marvellous,' he tells you, 'I am on the hill this very night to conduct an electrical experiment, and here you are with this wondrous creation all powered by the force I am investigating. You must tell me more.'

Bulkhead catches your eye and shakes his head.

'I'm afraid we cannot really discuss it,' he tells Franklin, reaching out to take the metal sphere from you.

He examines the ball carefully. 'These balls are the key,' he says.

'There were a couple of them missing,' you remember, thinking back to the time machine you found in Detroit. 'Could they be lost in the past?

If Benjamin Franklin tells you he has seen one, turn to 8.
If Benjamin Franklin tells you that he has not seen one, turn to 16.

Bulkhead does as instructed and keeps absolutely still.

You look around for a way to help the Autobots and spot something red fixed to the wall. You begin edging towards it. As you expected, the Decepticon only has eyes for the 'bots.

'Now slowly move away from the machine,' orders Blast-X. 'And I mean slowly. Any tricks and I'll shoot the organic.'

You realise with a start that he is talking about you.

'Where is the organic?' says Blast-X, now unable to see you.

Quickly you grab the fire extinguisher you've been moving towards and let it off in the direction of the Decepticon.

Fire-retardant foam shoots out of the nozzle and covers his face. He staggers and fires blindly, hitting the ceiling with a power blast. A section of the roof collapses.

If Bulkhead tells you to hide behind the time machine, turn to 23.

If Bumblebee attacks Blast-X, turn to 103.

Prowl agrees that you can ride with Bulkhead and soon you are back in his cab, speeding along the streets of Detroit, following Prowl in his motorcycle form.

Minutes later, you reach your destination. The rest of the Autobots meet you on the sidewalk in front of a large skyscraper set back from the street.

'According to our readings, the Professor is somewhere on the tenth floor,' says Ratchet, indicating the building.

You wonder why the Autobots haven't just gone in and captured the man.

Bumblebee laughs and spins around you. 'Do you really think we haven't tried that? Trouble is, he keeps using things snatched out of time to protect him.'

There is a sudden blast of hot air and a dense mist forms in the air. Something is coming through time.

If it is a horned dinosaur, turn to 24.
If it is a woolly mammoth, turn to 9.

The woman smiles broadly and then raises her voice. 'You can come in now, I have need of you.'

In response there is the sound of movement nearby. A giant robot crashes – literally – through the door, bringing much of the door frame, and the surrounding walls, with him as he makes his entrance.

'Say hello to Blast-X,' says the woman, laughing again. 'He's here to kill you.' She glances up at the giant robot who comes to stand at her side looking tough and invincible.

The newcomer points both his arms at Bulkhead and Bumblebee.

'Don't you know its rude to point?' says Bumblebee.

Blast-X ignores him and suddenly there is a deafening sound. A solid wall of sonic energy hits the Autobots with the force of a crashing tidal wave.

If the woman goes to the time machine, turn to 46.

If you step in her way, turn to 77.

You feel a sudden blast of heat coming from somewhere close by.

'Where's the fire?' you ask.

'Temporal energy spike,' shouts Bulkhead over the sudden wind that has come up from nowhere, 'like this wind, it's a side effect of a time portal.'

The time travelling nightmare that Bulkhead saved you from is enveloped in bright lights and a huge flash that temporarily blinds you. You blink and when the flashes fade you see that the street is now completely empty.

'So that's what it looks like to see one of these time-quakes,' you mutter, 'I wonder what's causing them?'

'I've got a trace on the energy so I might just be about to find out,' Bulkhead tells you. He then changes back into his SWAT car form.

If he suggests you jump in, turn to 100.
If he begins to drive off, turn to 89.

You feel Bulkhead running towards you and then his metal hand grabs you and you are pulled up into the air.

There is a flash of energy nearby and you feel a blast of hot air.

You realise that Bulkhead has just saved your life – some kind of energy distortion happened exactly where you were just standing.

Bulkhead puts you down gently.

'Are you alright?' he asks you.

'I'm okay, thanks,' you reply, 'but I don't know about him…'

You point at a figure that has appeared in the middle of the street at the exact point that the energy burst happened. You can see that the man is wearing a uniform you recognise from a school project.

'He's a Confederate Soldier,' you tell Bulkhead, 'from the American Civil War in the Nineteenth Century.'

If the man attacks you, turn to 102.

If he speaks to you, turn to 10.

Prowl pulls up next to you. 'You can ride with me,' he tells you.

At the Autobots top speed it doesn't take long to cover the short distance to the rendezvous point. Within a few minutes you are standing on a quayside with all five of the famous Autobots.

Optimus Prime briefs you all on the current situation.

'The Decepticon Wavelength and his prisoner are inside that building,' he tells you, pointing towards a single-storey restaurant which sits on a platform extending over the water.

'So why are you out here?' you ask.

'There is a problem,' Prime confesses.

'The Decepticon controls electricity. Every time we try and get near, we get our circuits scrambled,' explains Ratchet.

You tell them that you have an idea.

'My trainers have rubber soles,' you say, grinning.

'And that means you can get in!' says Bulkhead.

You explain your plan.

Turn to 53.

Without warning the man snatches the control ball from your hands and runs off.

'Hey! Come back!' you shout after him, but he has already disappeared around a corner.

'We have to get that back,' says Bulkhead, 'I'll change to vehicular mode to make the chase easier.'

'I don't think so,' you tell Bulkhead, 'have you seen the state of these roads? Your SWAT car form won't find them very easy. I'm sorry but we're going to be faster on foot.'

'Maybe next time you should time travel with Bumblebee,' complains Bulkhead, 'he's more use in a foot race than me.'

'Don't be too hard on yourself,' you tell the giant Autobot.

Bulkhead may not be as fast as Bumblebee, but he soon catches up with the thief.

If the man faints when Bulkhead picks him up, turn to 95.
If the man demands to be put down, turn to 83.

Bulkhead reaches out to grab hold of the bus. There is a terrific squealing and a smell of burning rubber as he applies his strength to stopping the bus.

You and Bulkhead escort the shaken girl to the safety of the pavement.

She is very grateful for your intervention. She tells you that her name is Gabriella Constanza. You gasp as you recognise the name. This girl is destined to be the first female President of the United States of America. You remember learning about her at school.

In her hand she has the object she ran into the road to fetch. To your surprise, it is a time machine control sphere.

You tell her that the sphere is yours and she hands it over to you.

If the sphere Bulkhead is holding lights up, turn to 78.
If the sphere you are holding lights up, turn to 42.

You find the floor beneath your feet giving way and you start to fall through. Prowl quickly bounds across the room and grabs you. He then tries to leap clear of the gaping hole that is forming beneath you but he is too far away from anything.

Held close by Prowl you fall into the dark cellar below.

Prowl lands like a panther, absorbing the impact with the shock-absorbers in his legs.

Bits and pieces of floor and ceiling shower down but Prowl bends over to protect you.

Bulkhead joins you.

'Are you alright?' he asks.

You tell him that you're fine. Prowl lets go and the three of you begin to explore the cellar further. It's a massive dark space and the orange glow you saw earlier is the only light.

If you lead the way, turn to 21.
If Bulkhead leads the way, turn to 99.

Bulkhead glances down at the strangely-dressed man. 'My main power source is electrical,' he replies.

'But that is incredible,' says Benjamin Franklin. 'I am conducting an experiment to prove that lightning is a form of electricity. But to power a mechanical man – how is that possible?'

Bulkhead looks at you and shakes his head.

'I can't really say,' you tell Franklin.

Bulkhead takes the metal control ball from you and examines it.

'This is the key,' he mutters. 'This both activates the travel and brings you back.'

As Bulkhead looked at the metal ball it begins to flash.

'Why is it doing that?' you ask.

'It's reacting to another control ball,' says Bulkhead.

'There was one missing,' you recall.

If Benjamin Franklin tells you he has seen one, turn to 8.
If Benjamin Franklin tells you that he has not seen one, turn to 16.

You are in the warehouse where you left Prowl but there is no sign of him in the room.

You and Bulkhead step off the time travel platform and begin to look for the ninja-like Autobot.

You look up as a movement catches your eye.

It's Prowl jumping down from what remains of the floor above.

'No need to scare us like that,' you tell him.

'Where have you been?' demands Prowl.

'We've only been gone a couple of hours,' you reply.

Prowl shakes his head. 'It's been days since you disappeared in that machine.'

'But where did the machine come from?' asks Bulkhead.

'And who's been using it?'

If Prowl tells you that a Decepticon is behind it, turn to 37.
If Prowl tell you that a Detroit scientist is responsible, turn to 59.

The figure steps clear of the dust cloud and you can see that it is a large robot – a Decepticon.

'Step away from the time machine,' orders the stranger.

The new arrival has some kind of pulse weapons fixed to both forearms.

'You didn't say "please",' Bumblebee tells him cheekily.

'My name is Blast-X,' the Decepticon tells him, 'and I don't need to.'

He raises his arms and points them towards the three of you.

Bulkhead steps forward protectively.

'You know, if you hit me with that force ray of yours again you'll send me right through that machine of yours,' Bumblebee points out, stepping to the side and placing himself directly in front of the time machine. 'I don't think you want to do that.'

'One more move and I will fire,' Blast-X warns Bulkhead.

If Bulkhead ignores him, turn to 28.
If Bulkhead keeps still, turn to 61.

President Lincoln steps forward.

'Where did you get that object?' he demands.

'I can't tell you,' you say, 'but you must trust me. The speech you are about to make will be inspirational, not just for the people here, but throughout this nation and the wider world – not just today, but for years to come.'

He stares at you wide-eyed.

'How can you say these things?'

'I cannot tell you. But you must believe me that if you have seen the twin of this object you need to tell me. Lives may depend on it.'

He looks at you for a long moment and then gives you a control ball from an inner pocket.

You pass it to Bulkhead who is standing close by.

If the sphere Bulkhead is holding lights up, go to 78.

If the sphere you are holding lights up, go to 42.

The massive lift hurtles towards the top of the building. When it reaches the top there's a melodic PING and the doors slide open.

You step out on to the entire top floor of the skyscraper. It's mostly empty, but at the far side of the vast cavernous space is some kind of strange machine.

There's a central metal box, surrounded by wires and cables. The box is four-sided, open at the top and the front. On a series of stands are a number of metallic spheres about the size of cricket balls.

When you step on to the platform to have a closer look, it lights up.

You start examining one of the balls.

'Don't touch anything,' says Bulkhead, reaching out to take the sphere from you.

If you are surrounded by a thick mist, turn to 94.
If you are enveloped in a bright blue light, turn to 20.

Bulkhead suddenly falls through the floor. He tries to stop himself by stretching his arms out, but only succeeds in pulling more of the floor down with him.

Now the whole of the floor is collapsing and you find yourself slipping towards a hole as the wooden floorboards buckle and crack.

Moving with incredible speed, Prowl leaps across the room and grabs you before making a final leap towards the concrete stairwell.

'Thanks,' you say, breathlessly.

Prowl is already hurrying down the staircase, taking the steps two at a time. You follow him and are soon emerging into a vast underground cellar. Much of the roof has collapsed, and under a pile of broken flooring and ceiling plaster you find Bulkhead.

If Bulkhead is unhurt, turn to 35.
If Bulkhead is hurt, turn to 45.

Suddenly the SWAT car begins to move. You gasp in amazement because there is no driver in the cab. You realise it must be a robotic car but then something amazing happens. Smoothly the car morphs into a familiar robotic figure.

It is Bulkhead, one of the Autobot heroes that defend Detroit from all kinds of evil. And he's here to help.

The powerful Autobot rips a water hydrant out of the ground, unleashing a fountain of water which flies into the air. Bulkhead then puts one of his massive feet into the flow of water, redirecting the jet directly into the face of the dinosaur.

The mighty Tyrannosaurus Rex is knocked off his feet.

If you feel something peculiar inside, turn to 40.
If you feel a blast of heat, turn to 64.

You step smartly between the woman and the machine.

'Get out of my way, youth,' she spits at you.

'You're not that old yourself,' you retort, as she tries to wrestle you out of the way.

'Don't let my looks fool you,' replies the woman, 'I'm four hundred and three years old.'

This surprises you so much you let her pass.

She leaps on to the machine platform and presses some controls on one of the spheres.

'Time for me to go,' she says.

'But who are you?' you demand.

'Where I come from, hundreds and hundreds of years from now, technology has become as advanced as magic. We want for nothing. But it's a sterile and boring life. I came here to seek some fun... That's all...'

Before your eyes the whole machine fades away and disappears.

If Bulkhead speaks, turn to 88.
If Blast-X speaks, turn to 29.

The sphere Bulkhead is holding lights up. A moment later, the one you are holding does the same.

Immediately the colour seems to drain from the surrounding area and nothing moves. It's as if time has frozen and drained all life and colour from everywhere except for a tiny spot occupied by you and Bulkhead.

'Here we go again,' says Bulkhead.

'Back to the future, or further into the past?' you wonder.

'I don't know,' confesses Bulkhead, 'but I hope there are no more of these spheres missing in the past. If something changes history, it could destroy our future.'

The now-familiar white light rapidly slides down over you, and your tummy lurches as you are plucked out of time and space.

If you have only visited one time zone so far, turn to 14.
If you have visited two different time zones now, turn to 49.

Blast-X completes his turn and finds Bulkhead looming over him.

CLANG! Bulkhead lays out the Decepticon with an old-fashioned right-handed punch.

'Pick on someone your own size next time,' says Bulkhead. But the Decepticon can't hear him – Blast-X is out cold.

'Good work team,' says a new voice. You see that the Autobot's leader, Optimus Prime, has arrived on the scene, along with Prowl and Ratchet.

Ratchet quickly crosses to examine the time machine.

'Looks like all the spheres have been recovered from the past,' he comments, 'that should put an end to the time distortions.'

'What? No more highway tag with real living dinosaurs?' complains Bumblebee with a smile. 'You guys take away all my fun!'

'We couldn't have done it without my young friend here,' says Bulkhead, bringing you forward to meet the rest of the team.

'So where did the machine come from?' you wonder.

Ratchet looks up. 'It seems to have fallen through time from the future.'

'And Blast-X?'

'Another of Megatron's many followers. He came across the machine and thought he could use it to bring us down.'

'How was he going to do that?' you wonder.

Prowl is securing the now recovering Decepticon with a pair of energy-negation handcuffs. You repeat the question and Blast-X looks at you disdainfully.

'The idea was to create chaos that the so-called heroes couldn't deal with, then I would have revealed myself and made the time-quakes stop. The Autobots would have been washed up and I would have stood in their place.'

'Yeah, great plan spanner head,' says Bumblebee, 'the only place you're going to be standing for a while is in your jail cell.'

Bulkhead suggests that its time to go home and wonders if you want to give the order.

'Transform and roll out,' you say.

YOUR ADVENTURE WITH THE AUTOBOTS IS OVER.

Prowl suggests that it might be safest if you travel with him and produces a safety helmet for you. Moments later you are out on the streets, riding on Prowl in his motorcycle form.

Soon you arrive at your destination – a skyscraper in the heart of the financial district.

Optimus Prime, Bumblebee and Ratchet are waiting and inform you that time energy signals are coming from the tenth floor.

'Why don't you just go in and get him then?' you ask the Autobots.

'You think we hadn't thought of that?' replies Bumblebee.

'Every time we make a move anywhere near the building, he time-scoops something from the past to stop us,' explains Ratchet.

'Mostly dinosaurs,' adds Prime.

Something begins to form in the air in between you and the building.

If it is a horned dinosaur, turn to 24.
If it is a woolly mammoth, turn to 9.

To your surprise, the woman starts laughing.

'You think I'm joking? Let me show you why I think you'll do as I say,' says Natasha.

She claps her hands and a massive robot clanks into view.

'Blast-X – remove these obstacles,' she orders.

Instantly the robot points his arms at Bulkhead and Bumblebee, and his wrists click open to reveal an energy weapon in each arm. BA-BOOM! The mysterious Blast-X unleashes some kind of sonic boom and completely takes Bumblebee and Bulkhead by surprise.

The blast of near solid sound rocks the Autobots and sends them flying. Bumblebee, being lighter, is sent flying towards a window. He smashes into the glass, but thankfully, it does not shatter.

Bulkhead slams into a corner of the room, damaging a supporting strut and bringing a section of the ceiling down on him.

If the woman goes to the time machine, turn to 46.
If you step in her way, turn to 77.

Benjamin Franklin leads you to the city of Philadelphia.

As you get closer to the buildings, you turn and look at Bulkhead.

'Perhaps you should wait here,' you suggest, 'you might cause a panic.'

Bulkhead does not like the idea. 'I don't want you left alone in the past,' he tells you.

'Fear not, man of metal,' says Benjamin Franklin, 'I will take care of the youth.'

You leave Bulkhead and follow Franklin into the city. It is very different from the Detroit you left. The buildings are mostly wooden and there are no cars, just wagons and horses.

When you reach his home, Franklin gives you the metal control ball he found.

You thank him and hurry back to Bulkhead.

When you get there, if the ball begins to glow, turn to 57.
If you give the ball to Bulkhead, turn to 19.

'Put me down sir, I demand it,' cries the man bravely.

Suddenly the control ball begins to bleep and flash again, this time at a faster pace.

'Let me take that,' suggests Bulkhead.

'There must be another sphere like this, somewhere close,' Bulkhead tells you.

The man rummages in his coat and produces a matching control ball.

'Pardon my actions friends, but when I saw the sphere I thought perhaps it was a charm. I hoped it would give me luck tonight.'

'Tonight?' asks Bulkhead.

'We are going to liberate the tea from the British East India Company's ships.'

'The Boston Tea Party!' you exclaim.

'Aye, it will be a party,' says the man. 'That's a great name for the endeavour.'

'An historic name,' you tell him with a grin.

If the ball he gave you begins to glow, turn to 57.
If you give the ball to Bulkhead, turn to 19.

You stare intently at the man, unable to believe your eyes. You've seen images of him in books and on screens but to actually meet him is incredible. The man looks up from his paper and sees you.

'Hail stranger, can I do you a service?' he says.

'Mr Lincoln?' you stammer. 'President Lincoln?'

He looks at you oddly, unused to being addressed so casually.

'That is my name,' he tells you.

Suddenly you realise where you are, remembering a TV movie you once saw. This must be the Soldier's National Cemetery in Gettysburg where Lincoln made one of the most famous speeches in history, the Gettysburg Address.

'You must excuse me sir, but I am due to make a short speech to dedicate this place of remembrance,' Lincoln tells you.

If you ask him about his speech, turn to 51.

If you ask him about the metal spheres, turn to 93.

The shock of time travel is a little less intense this time.

You look around, looking for clues to your spacial and temporal location.

You're standing in an alley between two tall wooden buildings. There's a scent of salty sea air and the sound of gulls. As you look out towards the light you see a sign pointing to "Griffin's Wharf".

Some strangely dressed men are creeping along the harbour road. They appear to be wearing old-fashioned Native American Indian costumes.

You grin as you realise exactly where you must be. And when!

'It's 1773,' you tell Bulkhead confidently, 'and we're in Boston watching the Sons of Liberty on their way to becoming famous.'

The metal control ball that you are holding starts to flash and make a sound.

If one of the men spots you, turn to 5.
If Bulkhead gets the ball to stop flashing, turn to 98.

You walk up to the vehicle.

'Hey!' you shout. 'Are you Bulkhead?'

In reply, there is a clanking, crunching sound and the SWAT car changes into a robotic figure you instantly recognise.

'There is danger here,' says Bulkhead, 'you should get away from this location.'

'What is it?' you ask, ignoring the Autobot's advice. 'Is it the time-quakes?'

'Time-quakes?' asks Bulkhead.

'The weird stuff that's been happening. The news channels are calling them time-quakes,' you tell the giant Autobot.

'I have realigned some internal sensors and have detected some temporal disturbance in this area,' says Bulkhead.

'Like I said – time-quakes,' you say with a grin.

Bulkhead begins moving towards the building.

'Whatever you want to call it, the centre of the phenomena is in there,' he says.

If you follow Bulkhead, turn to 15.

If someone comes out of the building, turn to 2.

Suddenly you feel something strange happening. It begins in the pit of your stomach and makes the hairs on the back of your neck stand up. Directly in front of you the air begins to heat up and shimmer.

You feel Bulkhead grabbing you and pulling you backwards.

'You need to get back, otherwise you'll end up lost in time, too,' he tells you.

There is an intensive flash of pure bright white light and you shield your eyes. Then the light fades and you realise that the time traveller has completely disappeared.

'I have a strong trace on the source of the temporal displacement. I think I can find whatever or whoever made this happen,' says Bulkhead.

Bulkhead changes into the SWAT vehicle again.

If he suggests you jump in, turn to 100.
If he begins to drive off, turn to 89.

'Fun?' he roars, furiously. 'She calls that fun? Dropping dinosaurs and cavemen from the past into 22nd century Detroit, destabilising history, causing chaos? Where's the fun in that?'

Another 'bot also roars, but this is a sound of anguish not anger. Blast-X cannot believe that the woman has abandoned him.

'Nooo!' he cries, falling to his knees.

'I guess she wasn't as keen on you as you hoped, eh pal?' says Bumblebee, trying to lighten the moment.

Blast-X turns on him and unleashes another of his sonic booms.

Bumblebee is sent flying.

'Hey, no need for that,' he calls as he flies backwards through the air.

Meanwhile Blast-X has got to his feet.

'She may have abandoned me, but she'll be back. And she left me with orders,' he remembers, 'so let's get back to it, right now.' With that, he attacks Bulkhead, but this time Bulkhead is ready. He reaches out and braces himself between two walls. The sonic boom hits him hard, but this time he is able to withstand it.

Blast-X points his arms to try again.

Before he can launch another sonic attack a metal axe slices though the air and chops off the ends of the enemy bot's arms. The two metal hands fall to the floor.

'Optimus Prime!' you call out, delighted to see that the Autobot leader has arrived.

Without the focusing units fixed to his hands, the sonic power of Blast-X cannot be directed. It feeds back on his own circuits and BA-BOOM! Blast-X knocks himself out.

You see that Ratchet and Prowl are also with Prime. Ratchet steps up and disconnects both of Blast-X's sonic canon arms.

'He's 'armless now,' jokes Bumblebee.

'I knew you were going to say something like that,' sighs Bulkhead.

YOUR ADVENTURE WITH THE AUTOBOTS IS OVER.

Bulkhead begins to drive off.

'Hey, what about me?' you shout after him.

To your surprise Bulkhead turns around in a sharp circle and pulls up next to you and the passenger door pops open.

'You'd better get in then, if you're coming,' Bulkhead tells you.

Before he can change his mind, you climb into the cab and buckle up. Bulkhead's voice fills the cabin as he takes off on the trail of the temporal energy – whatever that is. Bravely you ask him to explain.

'The time holes or time-quakes – whatever you want to call them – give off a peculiar radiation, an energy signal,' explains Bulkhead, sounding a little unsure about it himself. 'Ratchet built us a detector to trace the time energy whenever a fresh hole in time pops up. That's why I was there just now.'

'Like you were looking for time footprints,' you suggest.

'Yeah, you could call them footprints, I guess,' the friendly Autobot agrees.

'So where do they lead?' you ask.

Bulkhead flashes up a map on a screen inside the cab. On the map a blob flashes to indicate a particular block near the financial district downtown.

'It's a new building downtown,' he tells you. 'Just been finished, no tenants yet. At least, no official tenants.'

Bulkhead arrives at his target destination and comes to a halt. As soon as you get out he changes back into his robotic form.

'Let's take a look around,' he suggests.

The building is sleek with mirrored windows and has over eight storeys. The sign says it's Lions Tower.

Suddenly you see a movement in the shadows.

If someone jumps out, turn to 13.
If Bulkhead steps into the shadows, turn to 101.

The voice seems to come from an abandoned SWAT car that is standing in the street.

'Hurry,' says the voice again. You look back up the street and see that the Neanderthal – or whatever he is – is swinging some kind of weapon around his head. It looks like a sling. Suddenly he lets go and a heavy jagged rock zooms towards you.

At the same time, the SWAT car bursts into life. It changes into a familiar robotic form and you realise that it is Bulkhead, one of the Autobots.

He rips a parking sign out of the ground and swings it like a giant metal baseball bat.

CLANG!

He hits the caveman's projectile and sends it flying into the air over the caveman's head.

'Home run!' shouts Bulkhead, delighted.

If you feel something peculiar inside, turn to 40.
If you feel a blast of heat, turn to 64.

It really feels as if you are sinking into the floor but, in actual fact, it is not you that is sinking, but a wave of light is rising up from the floor and over your body. The light moves rapidly, but when it goes over your head, it suddenly disappears and you find yourself somewhere completely different.

'Where are we now – or should that be when?' you wonder, looking around curiously.

You are no longer standing inside at all; you and Bulkhead have materialised on a hillside.

Bulkhead nods. 'We need to know how far we have travelled in time and in which direction: backwards or forwards?'

'Well, it's daytime,' you say looking up at the sky, 'but it's either nearly sunset or there is a storm coming.' There are some dark clouds in the sky.

'But what is the year?' asks Bulkhead.

'There's a clue...' you say pointing down the hill where a man, dressed in old-fashioned clothes, is walking. He wears long socks, knee-length breeches, buckled shoes and a long coat. On his head, he has a wide-brimmed hat. He stops and looks at you – and Bulkhead – with astonishment.

'What is that? Some mechanical life?' he asks.

'His name's Bulkhead,' you tell the man, and then

you introduce yourself.

'Franklin,' says the man, shaking your hand, 'Benjamin Franklin at your service.'

Bulkhead flips open a panel on his arm and begins taking a reading. Benjamin Franklin steps closer and looks at the screen in fascination.

'What powers the script on that glass paper?' he asks.

If Bulkhead answers, turn to 70.
If you answer, turn to 60.

Bulkhead tries to scan for temporal energy.

'Great idea,' he tells you, 'but it's not working.'

'Why not?' you wonder.

Bulkhead shrugs. 'Must be this place. The pollution levels are very high.'

A little girl comes up to Bulkhead and pats his leg.

'Can you help me find my Daddy?' she says to Bulkhead.

Before Bulkhead can react, a worried-looking man runs up. 'Natalie, don't run off like that!' he tells the girl and drags her off.

The girl turns and waves at Bulkhead as they go. You notice a blur of action out of the corner of your eye. A teenage girl is dashing across the road, risking life and limb.

'Bulkhead! You're needed!' you shout out. A bus is about to hit the girl, who has now bent down to pick something up.

If Bulkhead grabs the runner, turn to 33.

If Bulkhead stops the bus, turn to 68.

'I need to ask you about something; have you seen anything like this recently?' you ask him. You hold out the metal ball but Lincoln is distracted. He stares off into space, muttering.

'I need a better conclusion. These words must inspire change and rebirth.'

Hearing him speak with this lack of confidence seems incredible. You know that this short but powerful speech will be remembered for centuries to come. You even had to perform it once in a school assembly.

'But the ending's great; "government of the people, by the people, for the people, shall not perish from the earth."'

Lincoln grabs a pen and notes down your words. 'That is brilliant. You have my gratitude.'

Ignoring the possibility that you've just created a time paradox, you ask Lincoln about the metal spheres again.

If President Lincoln calls an aide, turn to 17.

If Lincoln steps closer and whispers, turn to 73.

You are surrounded by a thick white mist that seems to rise up out of the platform you are standing on. Bulkhead takes the metal ball out of your hand.

You look around you, but it is impossible to see anything beyond the mist.

A wave of bright light is enveloping your body, rising up from the floor of the platform. It moves swiftly and soon you can feel it rising up your face. It's a weird sensation, like being tickled by a thousand tiny hands.

Then, as suddenly as it began, it is all over and you realise that the machine has completely disappeared and that you and Bulkhead are somewhere else.

Or some-when else.

Bulkhead takes a step forward and flips up a panel in his arm to enable him to read a sensor.

'Just some residual levels of temporal energy, but there's no way to know how far we've travelled in time,' he tells you. You take a look around.

'This is a cemetery,' you say, seeing there are simple white gravestones all around you. 'We won't get much information out of the dead.'

You begin to walk, threading your way through the lines of plain white crosses.

As you walk you can see the lines are actually

curved and the gravestones are arranged in semi-circles around some sort of monument. A crowd is gathered near the monument but you cannot make out any details of them. Between you and the crowd, a tall thin man is walking and muttering to himself. He has a distinctive beard that you instantly recognise.

If you call out the man's name, turn to 25.
If you stare at the man silently, turn to 84.

The man faints clean away. Bulkhead gently lays the man down on the ground.

'Take a look inside his coat,' suggests Bulkhead.

The man has a leather bag strapped around his body under his coat, and inside it you find another control ball.

You hold the two spheres in your hands.

'Look at that,' you say, 'he must have found one earlier.'

'I knew there had to be another one of them here,' says Bulkhead. 'Will the organic be alright?'

'He only fainted, he'll be fine. In fact, very soon he'll be famous,' you tell Bulkhead. 'The Sons of Liberty are about to take the tea from three ships from the British East India Company. We should take a look. This is the Boston Tea Party, live as it happens.'

If the ball you recovered starts to glow, turn to 57.

If you give a ball to Bulkhead, turn to 19.

You see a small window that is broken. 'If you can clear the broken glass out from that window, I think I can squeeze through.'

Prowl quickly removes the remains to the glass and Bulkhead picks you up so that you can scramble through. Once inside, you find a door and admit the two Autobots.

'Be careful,' you warn them, 'it looks like the floor is covered in holes, it might not be very strong.'

Bulkhead spots an orange glow coming up through one of the holes and Prowl moves agilely across the room to investigate. 'There's some kind of machine,' he reports. 'We need to get down to the next floor.'

'I don't think that's going to be a problem,' shouts Bulkhead as the floor creaks and groans under his weight.

If Bulkhead falls through the floor, turn to 75.
If you fall through the floor, turn to 69.

'This is the 21st century,' you tell Bulkhead.
'A hundred years before our time,' you add.

Bulkhead stares at you in amazement.

'How can you be so sure?' he asks.

You point towards a newsstand, where the date is clearly marked on the papers.

Bulkhead laughs.

'Oh, very good!' he says.

The control sphere gives off a bleep.

'There must be another one of these around here somewhere,' says Bulkhead. 'But where are we going to find it?' he continues. 'It's like looking for a needle in a haystack.'

He is right. There must be thousands of people on this block alone, not to mention all the drivers and passengers in the cars, buses and taxis on the roads.

'Can you scan for temporal energy?' you suggest.

If Bulkhead tries your idea, turn to 92.
If Bulkhead shakes his head, turn to 3.

Bulkhead takes the control ball from you and makes some adjustments using the buttons that are inlaid into the surface. The ball stops making its bleeping and flashing.

'There must be another of these control balls around here somewhere,' Bulkhead tells you.

'What devilry is that?' demands a husky voice.

You turn and see that you've attracted the attention of one of the "Native American Indians" making their way along the quayside. He steps closer to you and you can see that Bulkhead was right – the dark smudges on his face are coal dust.

'It's nothing to be afraid of,' you explain, 'it's a mechanical device, that's all.'

You take the ball from Bulkhead and hold it on your palm for the man to get a better look.

'It's harmless, see?'

If the man makes a run from you, turn to 32.
If he grabs the ball from you, turn to 67.

Bulkhead sets off across the room towards the machine that is making the orange glow.

The three of you begin to examine the machine.

It looks like a big open metal box. On the outside of the box are wires, dials and valves. Inside, there is a plain white platform and on the back wall there are a dozen indentations into which metal balls about the size of baseballs can be slotted. Two of the slots are empty.

You step inside and pick up one of the metal baseballs. It is surprisingly heavy and has three thick buttons and a couple of dials on it.

As you turn the metal ball in your hand the machine begins to power up.

Bulkhead hurries to join you.

If you begin to sink into the ground, turn to 91.

If you are enveloped in a bright blue light, turn to 27.

Bulkhead's passenger door pops open. 'Come on then,' he says.

You clamber in and the vehicle sets off. It's a little weird driving in a car without anyone being in the driver's seat but hearing Bulkhead's voice in the cab makes you feel a little safer.

'The energy trail leads to a location down by the river,' he tells you.

'Any idea who owns it?' you wonder.

'Its registered owners are a property development company, but I don't think they have anything to do with this time travel business,' explains Bulkhead.

'So who is behind it?'

'That's what we need to find out,' says Bulkhead coming to a halt in front of the building in question.

You get out of the cab and Bulkhead quickly changes his form again. The warehouse is old and full of broken windows. It sits on a spur of land sticking out into the Detroit River. Across the water you can see the lights of the Canadian city of Windsor.

'There's something round the side,' Bulkhead tells you, after scanning the building, 'let's take a look.'

He picks you up then leaps over the security fence, landing surprisingly gently on the other side.

Suddenly a figure emerges from the shadows.

'What kept you?' he says.

You see that it is another of the Autobots – the mysterious Prowl.

'I presume you followed the trail of temporal energy, too?' he continues.

Bulkhead nods. 'Must have been multiple time-quakes in different parts of the city.'

'Who's the kid?' asks Prowl, suspiciously.

Bulkhead looks at you. 'A friend,' he tells Prowl.

If you find a way in, turn to 96.
If Prowl leads the way, turn to 48.

Bulkhead steps into the shadows, reaches out and pulls up a figure that is skulking there. You see that he is now holding his fellow Autobot, Bumblebee.

'Hey! Get your paws off me!' says Bumblebee, but he seems more amused than annoyed.

Bulkhead releases him and the little yellow robot somersaults on to the ground.

'I was trying to blend in like a good spy,' he explains.

'I think you might need a new paint job to pull off a role like that,' says Bulkhead.

'Or a bright yellow wall to stand in front of,' you suggest.

Bulkhead asks his colleague what he has found out.

'The building's not let yet, so it's nearly empty,' Bumblebee tells you, 'but not completely empty.'

If he tells you that you need to go to the top floor, turn to 7.
If he tells you that he has found a way in, turn to 34.

The man suddenly rushes at you, brandishing his weapon and roaring wildly. Bulkhead quickly grabs you and hauls you out of his path. The time traveller tries to pull up and trips, falling flat on the ground.

You try to help him up but he backs away, crawling on the ground. You realise that the man is completely frightened. You try to reassure him.

'It's okay,' you begin, but the man interrupts, stammering with fear.

'Wh-wh-what is th-th-that metal th-th-th thing? Some Yankee wa-wa-war machine?' he demands, pointing a shaking finger at the Autobot.

'It's going to be okay,' you tell the solider, 'we can help. Can't we?' You address the last question to Bulkhead, who is busy checking some kind of scanner that is fixed to his arm.

If Bulkhead detects an energy spike, turn to 31.
If the soldier disappears, turn to 87.

Suddenly there is a flurry of energy blasts bouncing off the Decepticon's body armour. You realise that it is Bumblebee taking the attack to Blast-X.

A pile of masonry and other debris came down when Blast-X hit the ceiling and now he starts to use this material as improvised weapons, hurling chunks of metal and brick in the direction of Bumblebee.

You dash for cover behind the machine, while Bumblebee dances through the air, spinning and twirling and leaping to avoid the things that Blast-X is throwing at him

'I always said you were a great little mover,' says Bulkhead.

Blast-X lets the debris in his hands fall to the floor. He is aware that he has lost track of Bulkhead's position. Slowly he begins to turn to look behind him.

If Bulkhead is standing there, turn to 79.
If there is no one there, turn to 105.

The huge lift starts to go down.

'But I pressed up!' you complain.

'Security device?' suggests Bulkhead.

'Let's just override it,' says Bumblebee and zaps the control panel with one of his electric force blasts. Smoke pours out of the shattered cover of the control. Bumblebee puts a hand in, grabs the wires and ties some knots in them. 'Going up,' he announces.

When you reach the top floor, you discover an amazing machine.

There is a small platform big enough for two or three people, surrounded by wires, cables and generators. On the floor are a dozen indentations, most of which are filled by baseball-sized spheres. You step on to the platform and pick up one of the balls.

'Put it back!' says Bulkhead, but it is too late – something is happening.

If you let Bulkhead take the sphere, turn to 94.
If you hold onto the sphere, turn to 20.

Fearing the worst, Blast-X turns slowly but there is no-one behind him.

'Over here, lunk head,' says Bulkhead in a low rumble.

Blast-X spins around and sees that Bulkhead has managed to sneak around to the entrance. And he is not alone. Optimus Prime, Ratchet and Prowl stand with him.

'Take on one of us and you take us all on,' states Optimus.

He nods at Ratchet who immediately uses his magnetic powers to pull Blast-X off his feet.

Bulkhead strides forward and brings his two massive pile-driver fists down on either side of the robot's head. CLANG!

Blast-X hits the deck – down and out. A huge pile of dust is sent up into the air.

Meanwhile, Ratchet has crossed to check on the time machine.

'All in order here,' he reports. 'All the control spheres are back in place so that should be an end to any time disturbances.'

'That just leaves one thing to do, to ensure that this doesn't happen again,' says Optimus Prime. 'Bulkhead? Do your thing.'

Bulkhead attacks the machine. You remember that he was designed to be a destruction 'bot and you can see why. He reduces the time machine to rubble in less than a minute.

'I wonder where it came from?' you say when Bulkhead finishes his workout.

Blast-X is now restrained in some energy-sapping handcuffs. 'From the future of course,' he tells you. 'I thought I could use it to discredit you Autobots. When you couldn't stop the time-quakes, I would have, and then I'd have been Detroit's hero.'

'In your dreams,' you tell Blast-X. 'An idiot like you could never outsmart the Autobots.'

Optimus Prime laughs. 'Bulkhead – I do like your new friend!' he says.

He turns to look at you. 'Consider yourself an honorary member of the team!' he tells you.

YOUR ADVENTURE WITH THE AUTOBOTS IS OVER.

'Thank you for all your help,' Bulkhead tells you.

'It's been fun,' you reply. 'Maybe I can do it again some time?'

'Oh no,' says Bulkhead, quickly, 'I've had quite enough of time travel thank you very much. I think I get time travel sick!'

The rest of the Autobots wander over to join you.

'Are you sure that all the time distortions will stop now?' you ask them.

Ratchet nods. 'The time machine control spheres lost in the past were causing tears in the fabric of space-time that the dinosaurs, Neanderthals and other things were falling through. And the time-energy that released caused the fluctuations in the local time flow – all those rapid hours and very slow minutes – but now everything will go back to normal.'

'I bet school days still drag and holidays rush by,' you mutter.

The Autobots laugh. 'Like I said,' says Prime, 'everything is back to normal!'

YOUR ADVENTURE WITH THE AUTOBOTS IS OVER.